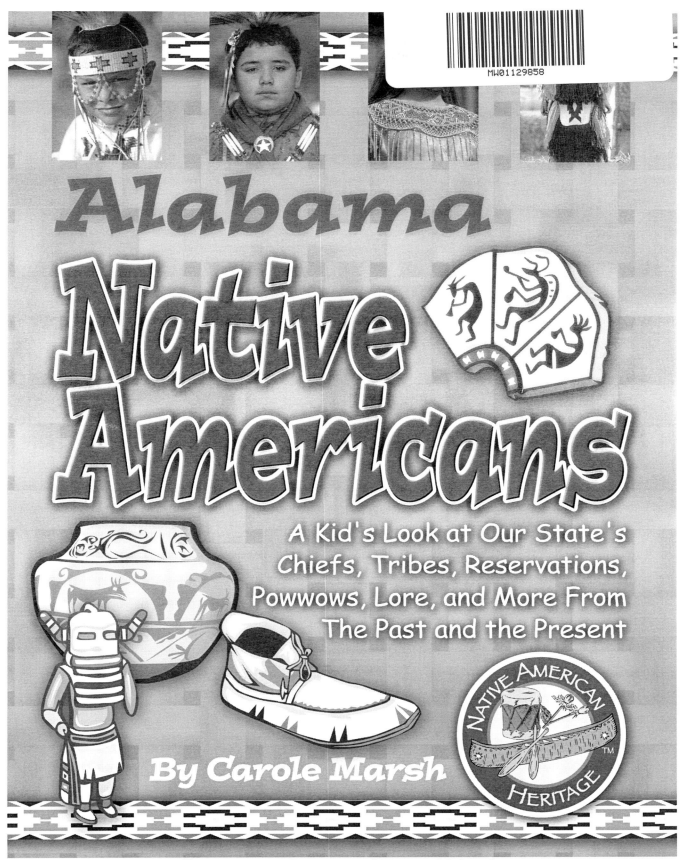

Alabama
Native Americans

A Kid's Look at Our State's Chiefs, Tribes, Reservations, Powwows, Lore, and More From The Past and the Present

By Carole Marsh

NATIVE AMERICAN HERITAGE ™

Editors: Jenny Corsey and Teresa Valentine
Graphic Design: Lynette Rowe • Cover Design: Victoria DeJoy

1

Published by

GALLOPADE™
INTERNATIONAL

800-536-2GET
www.gallopade.com

Gallopade is proud to be a member of these educational organizations and associations:

The National School Supply and Equipment Association
The National Council for the Social Studies
Association for Supervision and Curriculum Development
Museum Store Association
Association of Partners for Public Lands

Native American Heritage™ Series

Native American
Big Activity Book

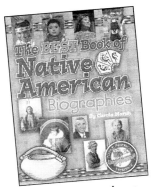

Native American
Biographies

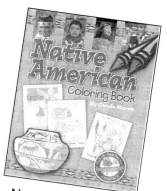

Native American
Coloring Book

Native American
Heritage Book

Native American
Timeline

Alabama STATE STUFF™

My First Pocket Guide: Alabama

My First Book About Alabama

Alabama Coloring Book

The Big Alabama Reproducible Activity Book

Jeopardy: Answers & Questions About Our State

Alabama "Jography!": A Fun Run Through Our State

Alabama Gamebooks

Alabama Bingoes

Alabama Illustrated Timelines

Alabama Projects

Alabama Bulletin Board Set

Alabama PosterMap

Alabama Stickers

Let's Discover Alabama! (CD-ROM)

Word from the Author

Hello!

I hope you are as interested in North America's wonderful Indian heritage as I am!

Like most kids, I grew up thinking of Indians as the other half of Cowboys. Today, of course, we are getting a much clearer and more accurate picture of what the first peoples on our land were all about. These "facts" are much more fascinating than anything Hollywood can make up. And you probably won't find much of this information in your history textbook!

I am 1/16 Cherokee. This is something I am very proud of and happy about. My grandmother was 1/4 Cherokee. She had tan skin, long gray hair and a very Indian look – especially if I did something bad! Her maiden name was Carrie Corn. Of course, when she got married, she took her husband's name, so it was many years before I learned to appreciate the significance of my native heritage.

Today, I'm trying to make up for lost time by exploring my roots as deeply as I can. One of the most interesting things I've learned is how fascinating all of the Indian tribes are – in the past, the present and future!

As you read about "your" Indians, remember that all native peoples were part of an ever-changing network of time, ideas, power and luck — good and bad. This is certainly a history that is not "dead," but continues to change – often right outside our own back doors! – all the time.

Carole Marsh
She-Who-Writes

PS: Many references show different spellings for the same word. I have tried to select the most common spelling for the time period described. I would not want to be in an Indian spelling bee!

4

Adze

An Indian woodworking tool used to cut, scrape, or gouge; often used to hollow dugout canoes. Blades were made of stone, shell, bone or copper.

Awl

An Indian's "needle." Often made from wood, thorns, bone, or metal, it was used to punch holes in skins so they could be sewn together.

Arrow

A long, slender shaft made of reed, cane, or wood; pointed tip was attached to one end and split feathers to the other. Feathers helped the arrows fly straight.

Alibamu or Alibama

Alabama's name comes from this tribe, which was the first Creek tribe to live in the region. They lived in small towns in log cabins. They farmed, fished, and hunted until white settlers and soldiers drove them west. Some still live in Oklahoma and in Texas.

Altar

A platform made of rocks or animal skulls; some had bowls, feathers, rattles, or skins on them. Indians prayed at these altars for things like good crops or expert hunting skills.

Arrowhead

The pointed tip of an arrow, made of bone, antler, wood, or iron. Some tips had barbs that would embed themselves in flesh. These barbs made it difficult for an enemy to remove the arrowhead from a wound.

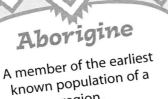

Aborigine

A member of the earliest known population of a region.

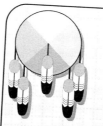

Abihka

One of the original Muskogee towns settled over 600 years ago, it was located along the upper part of the Coosa River. The Muskogee is a subtribe of the Creek tribe.

B is for . . .

"Bearers of the Red"

During wartime, the Creek Indians would erect tall red poles in the middle of their settlement. The warriors in charge of these poles were called "bearers of the red." When an Indian struck the pole, he was ready to fight!

Battle of Burnt Corn

The first battle of the Creek Indian War, which was fought on July 27, 1813. The Creeks won the battle, but their victory did little to prevent them from losing the ultimate war for their lands, which had been safeguarded by treaties.

Band

A subdivision of an Indian tribe. In earlier times, a band was sometimes created when part of a tribe split off from the main group. The band also chose new leadership.

Busk

Also called the Green Corn Dance, this event was held each year in late summer for 4-8 days. It was a time to make a fresh start. Everything was made new, from fire to clothing!

Baskets

Some were woven and others were coiled. Baskets were made from roots, grasses, barks, and other natural materials. Basketwork was also used for fences, fishnets, houses, mats, shields, cradles, and other useful items. Today Creek Indian women preserve these native folk arts by teaching others how to make baskets from white oak splints and straw. Such craft work is valued by people who realize how beautiful these ancient talents are.

Birmingham Museum of Art

Features archaeological exhibits about Alabama's Indians!

Burial

The Creek Indians traditionally buried their dead beneath the bed where the person had died.

Border Town

Original name of Talladega; site where General Andrew Jackson defeated a band of Creek Indians in 1813.

6

C is for . . .

Creek

A widespread and powerful nation of the Southeast. The Upper Creek lived mostly in Alabama. They built their villages along wooded rivers, creeks, and streams. The Creek were skilled farmers. Villages were organized into "red towns" for warriors or "white towns" for peacemakers.

Chunkey

Chunkey was a favorite game that the Creek tribe played. A stone disc was rolled down a court. Players ran behind and threw a pole, which was flattened at one end, close to where they thought the disc would stop. Each village had its own "chunkey yard."

Cherokee Phoenix

After the Cherokee Nation accepted Sequoia's alphabet in 1821, thousands of Indians learned to read and write in their own language–in just a few months! By 1828, the *Cherokee Phoenix* weekly newspaper was being printed in both English and Cherokee.

Choctaw

A tribe of excellent farmers and traders. It is believed that the Choctaw and the Chickasaw came to the South as one people and then separated. The United States used the Choctaw language as a special code during World Wars I and II.

Confederacy

A union of different groups of people. A confederacy in Indian culture was a group of tribes that agreed not to fight with each other. They agreed to live peacefully. Sometimes the tribes shared culture and language.

Chickasaw

Before the 1700s, the original Chickasaw main settlement was located on the Tennessee River east of Muscle Shoals. The Chickasaws were skilled warriors and hunters. They moved west to Mississippi when the Cherokees moved from the east.

Cherokee

One of the most famous southeastern tribes, they once roamed the mountains of Virginia, West Virginia, Tennessee, North Carolina, South Carolina, Georgia, and Alabama. The Cherokee sided with the English during the Revolutionary War, but did not participate in the battles. In 1827, they adopted a governmental system based on that of the United States called the "Cherokee Nation." For many years, the Cherokee lived in peace and shared respect with white settlers. When gold was discovered in their southeastern territory, the Cherokee were forced to leave their lands and move west. This tragic march was called the Trail of Tears.

7

Dead Men Tell These Tales!

When a member of the Choctaw Indian tribe died, his or her body was wrapped in skin and left outdoors until the flesh was almost gone. Respected tribesmen, who grew extremely long fingernails just for this purpose, picked the bones clean. The clean bones were put into a bone house. Mourning ceremonies were held at special times, and then the bones were buried.

Dance

There were Indian dances for every occasion: war, peace, hunting, rain, good harvests, etc. Drums, rattles, and flutes of bone or reed provided the music. Dancers often chanted or sang while performing. Steps were not easy to learn and required consistent practice.

Davy Crockett

Famous American hunter, trapper, and Indian fighter who served as a scout and guide under General Andrew Jackson during the Creek War. He died defending the Alamo mission during the 1800s.

Dinner Guests

The Alibamu Indians were very particular about entertaining Europeans. Following a meal shared with a white man, the Alibamu Indians would throw out all leftover food and wash everything the man had used!

Dishes

Made from clay, bark, wood, stone, and other materials, depending on what was available and what food they would be used for.

De Soto, Hernando

De Soto, a Spanish explorer, led the first expedition of Europeans through the Southeast in 1539. He killed or enslaved most of the natives that he met. His violent encounters eventually resulted in his death after just three years of exploration. News of his discoveries (riches and resources) prompted a host of Europeans to try their luck in the New World as well.

De Soto Caverns

Located near Childersburg, the caverns were discovered by Hernando de Soto in 1540. The Creek Indians hold this place sacred because their creation myth tells of spirits who rose from this cave to create their people. A 2,000-year-old Coopena Indian burial site, now on display, was excavated here in 1964.

Davis, John

European settlers took this Creek Indian prisoner when he was a just small boy. He later became a translator and worked with missionaries.

8

E is for . . .

Eagle

An animal used in many Indian ceremonies. Eagle feathers attached to war bonnets and shields communicated an Indian's rank in his tribe and what kinds of deeds he had done. Feathers also adorned rattles, pipes, baskets, and prayer sticks.

Eufaula

This Creek chief led his people out of Alabama in 1836 because they could no longer live safely and peacefully there. Before he left, Chief Eufaula visited the Alabama state capitol and talked with government representatives. He had come "to say farewell in brotherly kindness" to the people who had forced his people to leave. The town of Eufaula, Alabama is named in honor of this humble chief.

Earrings

Medicine men sometimes pierced male and female ears at special ceremonies. Earrings, which cost parents or relatives a significant amount, symbolized wealth and distinction. The more earrings that an Indian wore, the greater his honor. Some earrings measured 12 inches in length!

Epidemics

Few Indians possessed immunity to the deadly diseases, like smallpox and measles, which European explorers and settlers brought to the New World. As a result, great population loss took place. Sometimes entire tribes became extinct. Epidemics sparked by Hernando De Soto's expedition are estimated to have killed 75% of the native population in the New World.

English

In the 1800s, the U.S. government built boarding schools for Indian children throughout the nation, including the Southeast. Children were forced to leave their homes and families to live at these schools. They were required to learn English and not speak their native languages.

Fetish

These small objects were thought to hold the spirit of an animal or a part of nature. A fetish could be an object found in nature, such as bone or wood, or it could be a carved object. The fetish was usually small enough to be carried in a small bag or on a cord. The making and use of a fetish was kept secret by its owner and only shared with the one who inherited it.

Farming

Alabama Indians grew maize (corn), beans, pumpkins, sweet potatoes, peas, and sunflowers. The Creek welcomed the corn harvest, their most important crop, with the Green Corn Ceremony. Many different Indian dishes were made from corn. It was also dried so that it could be stored and eaten during the winter.

Florence

Creek, Cherokee, Chickasaw, and other Indian tribes once lived near this Alabama town. The first white settlers here leased land from Chief Doublehand as early as 1807.

Fort Mims

On the afternoon of August 30, 1813, hostile Creek Indians called Red Sticks massacred between 250 and 400 settlers. This event sparked a yearlong war called the Creek War, or The Great War. The massacre site is now located near Baldwin County in southern Alabama.

Fort Jackson

Andrew Jackson built this fort during the Creek War in 1813-1814. A recreation of this fort can be seen at a park just outside Montgomery.

Fire Drill

A device used by Indians to make fires which consisted of a stick and a piece of wood with a tight hole in it. The stick was twirled rapidly in the hole, creating friction that would ignite shredded grass or wood powder placed nearby to start a fire.

Fort Toulouse

The French built this fort to control trade with the Creek Indians. Creek leader Red Eagle signed a peace treaty with Andrew Jackson here which ended the Creek Indian War. A recreation of this fort now lies near Wetumpka.

Five Civilized Tribes

European settlers dubbed the Seminole, Choctaw, Chickasaw, Creek, and Cherokee the Five Civilized Tribes. After these tribes had been moved to Indian lands west of the Mississippi, they lived peacefully, farmed, and maintained governments similar to the colonial government. These actions made them "civilized" in the settlers' eyes.

 **is for . . .**

Green Corn Ceremony

This important annual Creek celebration took place in either July or August, depending on the harvest, and lasted up to 8 days. Other southern Indians observed this sacred event as well. During the ceremony, people settled arguments, gave thanks for the harvest, performed the green corn dance and began a new year.

Games

Adults played ball and other games of chance or skill. Indian children spun tops, fought pretend battles, did target-shooting, walked on stilts, played hide and seek, or competed to see who could hold their breath the longest! Creek Indians loved to play ball.

Gorgets

Beautiful ornaments hung around the neck or from ears; their significance, if any, is unknown.

Gourds

Hollowed-out shell of a gourd plant's dried fruit which often grew into a specific shape. Indians raised many species of gourds. They were used for spoons, bowls, masks, rattles, and even storage.

Great War

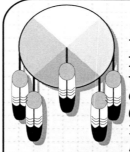

This conflict began in 1813 when the Creek Indians decided to stop the Americans from taking their land. A hostile faction of the Creek tribe, called the Red Sticks, began the Great War by attacking Fort Mims in August of 1813. Responding to the massacre, General Andrew Jackson led American troops in a series of battles against the Creek Indians. The war ended at the Battle of Horseshoe Bend on the Tallapoosa River in Eastern Alabama, on March 27, 1814. General Jackson's troops killed most of the remaining hostile Creek Indians during this battle.

 **is for . . .**

Hatchet

A small, short-handled ax, primarily used as a tool, not as a weapon. When settlers moved in, stone hatchets were replaced with iron ones.

Hair

Indians used hair as a textile. Hair from bison, mountain sheep, elk, moose, deer, dog, rabbit, beaver, or even humans were used to weave cloth, make wigs, or stuff pillows, balls, dolls or drumsticks.

Horn and Hooves

Indians used animal horn to make spoons and dishes. Hooves were made into rattles and bird beaks were used for decoration.

Head Flattening

The significance of this Choctaw custom, flattening the heads of young children, remains unknown. Experts say flat heads might have symbolized beauty or higher social standing. Parents laid their babies in hinged cradle boards to press their skulls or against boards with weighted leather strips.

Homes, Sweet Homes

Most Creek Indians had a winter home and a summer home in the same village. The winter home was thatched with bark or grass and built around a central fire. Summer homes were oblong buildings arranged around an open fireplace.

Horseshoe Bend National Military Park

This historic park near Dadeville marks the site where the final battle of the Creek Indian War took place.

Hiaphlako

Two Upper Creek Indian towns in Macon County bear this name, which means "tall cane."

Horse Pens 40

Creek Indians used this natural semi-circle rock formation in Steele, Alabama to catch and corral wild horses. The number 40 indicates that the place is 40 acres in size. Today Horse Pens 40 is a nature park, where many bluegrass music festivals are held.

Happy New Year!

On the first day of the new year, Creek priests placed four logs in a cross shape and lit a new and sacred fire in the center of town. Women of the tribe came to take away burning embers to provide their families with a new fire for the coming year.

 is for . . .

Ikanatchati

Once a village of the Creek, specifically an Alibamos tribe, the Ikanatchati stood along the Tallapoosa River, where Montgomery lies today. The word means "Red Ground."

Indian Removal Act of 1830

This federal act gave President Andrew Jackson the power to relocate tribes east of the Mississippi to an "Indian Territory." The forced removal of the southeast Indians later became known as the "Trail of Tears."

Indian Mound and Museum

Located in Florence, this site features the largest ceremonial Indian mound in the Tennessee River Valley. The archaeological museum also offers a large collection of Indian artifacts.

Indian Territory

The Choctaw, Cherokee, Creek, and Chickasaw Indians were removed to Indian Territory, which lay west of the Mississippi River. The U.S. government originally gave the many tribes approximately 19 million acres as a permanent home. Several bills to establish it were introduced in Congress, but none were enacted, though removal was already taking place. Over time, the "territory" shrank and split up. What was once supposed to cover two entire states and parts of three more states was reduced to roughly the southeast half of present-day Oklahoma by 1890. The remaining land eventually evolved into Indian reservations or Indian trusts.

Indian Ladder

Indians made ladders by trimming branches off a tree. Some were left at consistent intervals to provide steps.

Indian

In 1493, Christopher Columbus called the native people he met in North America "Indians" because he mistakenly believed he had sailed to India! Today, this term includes the aborigines of North and South America.

Indian Scout

This term, used to describe a guide, applied to Indians or Europeans.

13

J is for . . .

Junaluska

Cherokee chief Junaluska fought with General Andrew Jackson against the Creek Indians at the battle of Horseshoe Bend. He and two other warriors braved enemy fire to steal Creek war canoes at night for the Americans. Their mission helped General Jackson, who had been losing, to win the battle. During the fighting, Junaluska also killed a Creek Indian who nearly killed General Jackson. Years later, when General Jackson became U.S. president, he ordered the Cherokee to leave their lands. Junaluska pleaded with him to spare his people the Trail of Tears journey. But President Andrew Jackson told him, "There is nothing I can do for you."

Jesuits

Roman Catholic priests called Jesuits were among the first to meet and live with the North American Indians. Their writings, sent back to Europe, serve as one of today's best references to early Indian life.

Jefferson, Thomas

Early U.S. president who helped coin the "red man" description of Indians.

Judicial Termination

Modern term to describe current efforts by various U.S. government agencies and officials (especially the judicial system) to legally decrease the sovereignty of independent Indian tribes.

Jackson, General Andrew

Military and political leader who organized American militia and even some Indians to fight the Creeks, a war which sparked in Alabama. Later as U.S. president, he helped force Indians to relocate and give up their land with deceptive treaties. He also convinced Congress to ratify a treaty which led to the "Trail of Tears" exodus.

Jerked Meat

Thin strips of buffalo, elk, deer or other animal meat which is dried on racks in the sun; also called "jerky."

Kawita

A former Lower Creek village on the Chattahoochee River in Russel County, Kawita was called "bloody town" because anyone taken captive by the Creek warriors who lived there was put to death.

Kitchopataki

An Upper Creek town on the Tallapoosa River in Randolph County, Kitchopataki means to "pound grain."

Koasatis

Also spelled Coushatta or Quassarte, this tribe was closely tied to the Alibamos. They settled on the banks of the Alabama River. Later some of them moved to join the Alibamos farther west. Those who stayed became part of the Creek confederacy.

Knots

Tied on bowstrings, spearhead and arrowhead lashings, snowshoes, and other items, knots were sometimes used to keep track of the days like a calendar—each knot equaled 1 day.

Knife

Made from various materials such as bone, reed, stone, wood, antler, shell, metal, or animal teeth (bear, beaver, etc.), knives were used as weapons but also creative handiwork.

Killed Pottery

Pottery placed in a grave as an offering to the dead person was called killed pottery. A hole was formed in its base during creation. Often broken pottery was placed in a grave because Indians believed the spirit of the dead person would then be released and could travel.

L is for . . .

Linguistic Families

There are 56 related groups of American Indian languages. A few of these speech families include Iroquoian, Algonquian, Siouan, Muskogean, Athapascan, and Wakashan.

Leggings

Both men and women wore cloth or skin covering, which were often decorated with quills, beads, or painted designs, for their legs.

Lost Tribes of Israel

This historic theory has been floating around since 721 BC. The 10 lost tribes of Israel are supposedly groups of people gathered together by Sargon, the King of Assyria. Some say he cast out 10 of the 12 tribes of Israel. Many have tried to prove that the American Indians are these missing tribes!

Legends

Historic stories or myths passed down through the generations.

Land Rights

Before the Creek War (1813-1814), the Indians sold the rights to their land along the Atlantic Coast to Governor James Oglethorpe and the Colony of Georgia. After the war, the Creek Indian tribes were forced to move to the Indian Territory west of the Mississippi River. How much land did the Creek Indians give up? Their territory was about half the size of present-day Alabama!

Like, With an Attitude?

The Creek Indians of Alabama were considered to be very proud, even haughty and arrogant, but also very brave!

Lodge

A term for any type of Indian house that usually meant a permanent dwelling. The population of a tribe was often estimated by its number of lodges.

Lance

Spear used for hunting and war. The hunting lance had a short shaft and a broad, heavy head. The war lance was light and had a long shaft.

Lacrosse

The French named this popular Indian game played with webbed sticks and a ball. Indians of different regions of the country played slightly different versions of the game, but it was an important part of culture to all Indians. Southeastern Indians sometimes played the game to settle land disputes between tribes, sometimes up to 100 points. The men's games were followed by the women's games.

Lariat

These throw ropes made of rawhide, buffalo hair, or horsehair sometimes measured up to 20 feet long!

16

Mound Builders

The prehistoric Indian tribes who inhabited the eastern part of the United States built huge earthen structures with sophisticated building techniques. The reasons for building these mounds are still a mystery, but archeologists say they were probably used for ceremonies, for burial grounds and for meeting places.

Menewa

A Creek Indian chief, known for his opposition to Indian removal, who fought at Horseshoe Bend in the Creek War. He was defeated by the American troops. He lived despite being left for dead after suffering eight bullet wounds.

Muskogean

A family of Indian languages spoken in the southeastern U.S.; members of any tribes that spoke Muskogean are referred to as Muskogean. The Choctaw, Creeks, Chickasaw, and Seminole are part of this group.

Mingos

Chickasaw chiefs were called mingos, which means "treacherous."

Mound State Monument

A prehistoric Indian settlement and ceremonial center in Moundville. It is the largest mound site in the South. The site also includes a reconstructed Indian village and a museum with excavated Indian burials.

Moundville

Located south of Tuscaloosa, the site features approximately 40 burial mounds that were built about 800 years ago. The largest mound measures 58 feet in height and nearly 2 acres! Artifacts unearthed here show that the Moundville people knew how to make pottery, carve stone, and create copper ornaments.

Maubila

This extinct tribe, led by Chief Tuscaloosa, was remembered for their battle at Maubila against explorer Hernando de Soto. The Indians wounded nearly every man who was not killed, so the battle became a turning point of de Soto's expedition. However, the Indians, who suffered massive losses themselves, were wiped out by the Spanish soldiers. The location of this battle may have been between the lower Alabama and Tombigbee rivers.

 **is for . . .**

Native Peoples

The present-day state of Alabama has been inhabited for thousands of years. Many of these inhabitants were killed by war or disease brought by European explorers and settlers. However, in recent years, the Indian population in America is increasing. Today more than 16,000 Indians live in Alabama, according to the U.S. Census of 2002.

Nation

There are many Indian nations that live within the United States, such as the Choctaw Nation or the Cherokee Nation. Indian nations are called nations because their governments and laws are independent of and separate from the U.S. government. The federal government must have "government to government" relations with these Indian nations, just as it would with foreign nations, like England or Spain.

Nuts

This type of food was extremely important to the Native American diet. In the Southeast, Indians collected chestnuts (which are now nearly gone because of the 1905 chestnut blight), pecans, hickory nuts, black walnuts, and acorns. These nuts could be cracked and eaten raw, stored in their shells, and preserved for winter. They were delicious!

Names

Indian names were often changed during one's lifetime. These names could be derived from events that happened during the person's birth, childhood, adolescence, war service, or retirement from active tribal life. Some names came from dreams, some were inherited, and sometimes names were stolen or taken in revenge. Today some Indians maintain old, traditional Indian names, while others take modern names. Since settlers often did not read or write Indian languages, they recorded Indian names phonetically (as they "sounded"). Thus Indian names were often misspelled.

Noccalula Falls

A 90-foot waterfall near Gadsden is named for a legendary Indian princess. According to legend, Noccalula was a beautiful young Indian girl who was to marry a wealthy chief of another tribe. Noccalula did not care for the chief; she loved a young brave of her own tribe. Her father, who had arranged the marriage, stubbornly refused to change his mind. On the day of her wedding, Noccalula left the festivities and walked to the falls alone. There she leapt to her death. Her heartbroken father named the falls after his daughter, who never returned to her grieving lover.

18

Osceola

This famous Seminole chief and warrior fought furiously against the U.S. government when his tribe was ordered to move to the Indian Territories in 1830. He also influenced his people with his great speaking skills. A portrait of Osceola hangs in the Arlington Antebellum Home in Birmingham.

Old Mad Town

A Creek village that once existed near Birmingham.

Oakfuskee

A large Creek village on the Tallapoosa River in Cleburne County.

Ocheese Creek

The Creek Indian tribe got its name from settlers who came to the Carolina colony. They called the tribe of Indians that lived on the Ocmulgee River banks in Alabama "Ocheese Creek." This means "those who live on the creek."

Osotchi

Lower Creek town on the Chattahoochee River in Russell County.

Oil

Indians extracted oil from the many layers of fat that came with fresh bear meat. The fat was boiled down in earthen pots to produce the oil, which was stored in gourds and pots. The oil was used for cooking and even beautifying the body! Indians would mix red pigment with the oil, add the fragrances of cinnamon and sassafras, and rub it all over their bodies.

Orators

Many Indian leaders were excellent public speakers. Powerful and dramatic speakers were vital to leaders who wanted to influence their tribe. Watch for famous Indian quotations in literature and textbooks! One example is Creek Chief Eufala. Before he led his people west to the land the U.S. government reserved for them, he visited the Alabama state legislature to say goodbye. This is what he said:

"I come here, brothers, to see the great house of Alabama and the men who make the law, and to say farewell in brotherly kindness before I go to the far West, where my people are now going. In these lands of Alabama, which have belonged to my forefathers and where their bones lie buried, I see that the Indian fires are going out. Soon they will be cold. New fires are lighting in the West for us, they say, and we will go there. I do not believe our Great Father means to harm his red children, but that he wishes us well. We leave behind our good will to the people of Alabama who will build the great houses and to the men who make the laws. This is all I have to say."

Powwow

The original form of the word meant "medicine man." Medicine men would often use noise motion and confusion to scare away harmful spirits and cure people. It was also a gathering to talk about political matters. Today, the powwow is an event where Indians gather to sing, perform ceremonial dances, and share cultural pride and traditions.

Pearls

Southeastern Indians used pearls for decoration and in burial ceremonies. Hernando de Soto dug up many Indian graves to steal the pearls that had been buried there.

Plates

Notched stone plates have been found in Alabama Indian mounds. They may have been used to grind pigments to make paint. Some plates features bird, snake, or other designs.

Paint

Indians used many natural materials to make paint, like clay mixed with bear grease. Yellow "paint" was made with the gall bladder of a buffalo! Why did they paint their faces or bodies? Indians used paint to look scary or beautiful, to disguise themselves, or to protect their skin from sunburn or insect bites. Indians often applied red paint because it symbolized strength and success. That is why settlers often referred to the Indians as Red Men.

Pemmican

Indian food made of animal meat, which was dried in the sun, pounded together with fat and berries. The mixture was packed into skin bags and used primarily while on the trail.

Papoose

An American Indian infant aged between birth and one year is called a papoose. This word also refers to the way infants were bundled and carried by its mother. A papoose spent most of his or her days snugly wrapped in a kind of cradle made of skins or bark and a wooden frame that hung on the mother's back. This sturdy frame also allowed a mother to lean her papoose against a tree or rock within sight as she worked.

Pottery

Indian pottery was made from built-up spirals of clay that were molded or paddled, or a combination of the two methods. Most pottery served as cooking vessels.

Picture History

Some Indians kept a record of time and important events by painting or drawing pictures or symbols on skin, bark, or stone.

20

Quillwork

Indians used the quills of porcupine or birds to make a type of embroidery. Quills were dyed with juice from berries and other materials. When they were ready to be used, the quills were either mashed with teeth or softened with hot water and flattened with rocks. The quills were then laced into moccasins, shirts, pipe covers, and other items. Beads which Indians received by trading with settlers eventually replaced quillwork.

Quarry Site

A place where Alabama Indians would go to find malleable stone, such as flint, for tools.

Quiver

Case used to hold arrows; made of woven plant materials or animal skins.

Quirt

A short riding whip with a wood, bone, or horn handle.

Quad Site

An important archaeological site on the Tennessee River across from the city of Decatur. Digs showed that early Alabama Indians used this area for campsites.

Reservations

The U.S. government set aside, or "reserved," land for the Indians. These reservations originally served as a sort of prison during the beginning stages of Indian removal. At that time, reservations provided the government with some control over Indian activity and residency. This land was usually considerably less desirable land than the Indians' native territories. Today's reservations are lands that are tribally held, yet protected by the government. And the people are free.

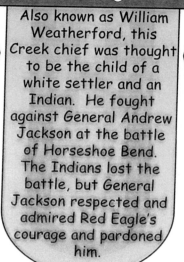

Red Eagle

Also known as William Weatherford, this Creek chief was thought to be the child of a white settler and an Indian. He fought against General Andrew Jackson at the battle of Horseshoe Bend. The Indians lost the battle, but General Jackson respected and admired Red Eagle's courage and pardoned him.

Rain Dancing

The rain dance ceremony, performed to encourage rainfall, was common among Indian religions because good weather is vital for a successful harvest. Rainmakers were in tune with nature; there are actual reported cases of Indians producing or preventing rain!

Roots

Indians used plant roots for food, medicine, dye, baskets, cloth, rope, salt, flavoring, and just to chew!

Red Sticks

A warrior faction of Creek Indians that lived in "red towns" was named Red Sticks by the settlers because of their red war poles. In the early 1800s, the Red Sticks and White Sticks warred with each other because of their different relations with settlers. The resulting war ended with the battle at Horseshoe Bend. General Andrew Jackson punished the Creek by forcing them to sign a treaty that gave up 23 million acres of land from both sides, even though the White Sticks supported General Jackson!

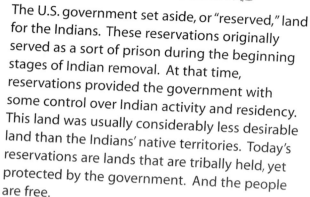

Russell Cave National Monument

Located near Bridgeport, this cave was home to the earliest-known human inhabitants of Alabama. It is thought to have been inhabited continuously for about 8,000 years, starting around 7,000 BC. The main room measures about half as long as a football field!

 **S is for . . .**

Slaves

Wealthy Indians sometimes owned slaves, who were later removed to the Indian Territory along with their owners and often freed. During the 1500s explorations of Hernando De Soto, many Southeast Indians became slaves themselves. De Soto routinely forced them into slavery on his expeditions. He also captured Indians and shipped them off to sell on the slave market. Indians also enslaved each other, especially during conflict. War captives became slaves, often to replace tribal members lost in the fighting.

Sacred Fire

Each Creek head town extinguished and re-lit their sacred fire during the annual Green Corn Ceremony. A high priest performed the re-lighting, the most sacred part of the busk. Then every household fire was started anew from the sacred fire. The sacred fire was the earthly symbol of their god, the Breath Maker.

Sawanogi

Creek and Shawnee town located in Macon County, around 1773.

Shawnee

Though the Shawnee were primarily a nomadic tribe, several lived in Alabama for hundreds of years. When President Andrew Jackson forced many Indians to move west, some Alabama Shawnee refused to go. The Piqua Sept of the Ohio Shawnee in Ider, Alabama, were granted official tribe status by the state of Alabama in 2001.

Stanfield-Worley Bluff Shelter

Archaeological site near Tuscumbia. Digs have shown that native people used the spot from the earliest times until about 1500 AD.

Stickball

The Choctaw loved to play stickball, their version of lacrosse. Often entire villages would participate in a game. They needed the whole village because sometimes a "team" could be comprised of as many as 60 people! Choctaw called the rough game was called the "little brother of war" because many players were injured, sometimes even killed, during play.

Sequoyah

Sequoyah was born in the late 1700s to a white father and a Cherokee mother. After moving to Alabama, Sequoyah injured his leg in a hunting accident. The injury bothered him for life and forced him to pursue a sedentary lifestyle of study. Sequoyah created an alphabet for the Cherokee language so that it could be written down. His achievement was a historical first. In 1821, the leaders of the Cherokee Nation approved his alphabet. Soon many tribe members learned to read, write, and publish in their own language, skills which helped them to better relate to Americans.

T is for . . .

Tribe

A group of Indians with shared culture, history, original territory, ancestry, social organization, and governmental structure. A tribe may contain several bands of Indians.

Tohopeka

Creek village where American militia killed 500 Indians in 1813 during the Creek War.

Trail of Tears

In 1838, the U.S. government troops rounded up Southeastern Indians and made them walk to Indian Territory west of the Mississippi River. Thousands of Indians died during this disastrous trek. Indians later named their historic march the Trail of Tears.

Tuskegee

A small village of Upper Creeks located in Elmore County, Alabama. The name originates from the Creek word for "warrior."

Tukabatchi

Upper Creek village located near present-day Talassee. The Shawnee Indian Chief Tecumseh met there with the Creek chief when Tecumseh was trying to organize all the Indian tribes to fight against the U.S. The Creeks did not want to join Tecumseh in his fight. When he left, Tecumseh vowed to stamp his foot when he got back to the North and cause Tukabatchi to crumble. Several days later, on December 16, 1811, the whole country experienced a major earthquake caused by a slippage of the earth's plates. But the Creek of Tukabatchi were convinced that Chief Tecumseh had caused it!

Talapoosa

At least 13 Creek towns were given this name!

Tattoos

The Creek and Cherokee tribes tattooed young boys when they were named and again when they became warriors.

Talladega

This Upper Creek Indian town along the Coosa River was the site of an 1813 battle between U.S. soldiers and Creek Indians. The battle was part of the Creek War of 1814-1814, which was fought between Indians and the American settlers who wanted their land.

Tuscaloosa

This town's name, which was also the name of a famous Maubila chief who tangled with Hernando de Soto, means "Black Warrior" in Choctaw.

U is for . . .

Universities
Study Native Americans at Auburn University in Auburn and the University of Alabama in Tuscaloosa!

Upper Creeks

A division of the Creeks who lived along the Coosa and Tallapoosa Rivers in northeastern Alabama.

U.S. Bureau of Indian Affairs

Provides public services such as law enforcement, land records, economic development, and education to Indians. Known for mismanagement and ethical problems.

U.S. Indian Reorganization Act
Passed by Congress in 1934, the act authorized Indian tribes to establish and conduct their own governments, and to form businesses.

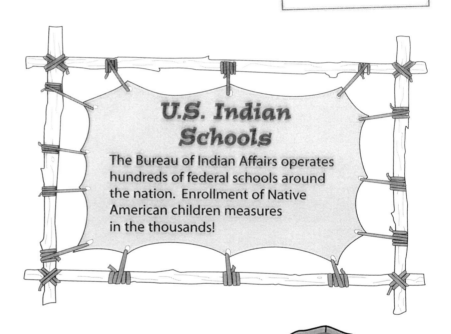

U.S. Indian Schools
The Bureau of Indian Affairs operates hundreds of federal schools around the nation. Enrollment of Native American children measures in the thousands!

U.S. President

Once called Great White Father by Indians.

U.S. Colonists
Called Long Knives or Big Knives by early Indians, who also called English explorers "Coat Men."

U.S. Indian Wars
The U.S. War Department has compiled an official list of "Indian Wars" that occurred in the United States. Over 50 wars were fought between the U.S. and the Indians during the period of 1790-1850.

Vessels

Indians carried water in special gourds shaped liked bottles, called water vessels.

Village Councils

These were held in the town (council) house and occurred to discuss and decide important matters. Harmony and agreement was essential to tribal unity. Rather than vote on issues, they were discussed until everyone was satisfied. Anyone who wanted to could speak freely. Everyone did not always agree on the outcome, but everyone avoided conflict by pushing their case.

Vegetable Dyes

Indians could not buy color from the store like we can today. Instead, they created many different colors from the things they found on earth like plants, flowers, shrubs, trees, roots, and berries. They made beautiful and unique reds, oranges, yellows, greens, browns, and violets. These dyes were used for baskets, pottery, weaving, body makeup, and clothing.

Valley Head

An important Cherokee center before the arrival of white settlers where a spring rose. Sequoyah, who lived near here and invented the Cherokee alphabet, is remembered with several historic markers.

Villages

Southeast Indian villages had a large central courtyard around which houses stood. The courtyard was used for gatherings and celebrations. Leaders and villagers met in a council house. Many villages had an athletic yard where the village could play stick ball.

 # W is for . . .

Worst Battle

The Maubila, led by chief Tuscaloosa, versus Hernando de Soto in 1540 fought one of the bloodiest Indian-European fights in American history. Though the town was well fortified, the Spanish armor and horses proved a successful advantage. More than 2,500 Indians were killed.

Weapons

The Creek Indians made blowguns from cane. Hunters often stalked deer using deer-headed decoys. Sometimes Indians fished by poisoning the water with roots that would drug the fish!

Wattle and Daub

A method of building houses using a pole framework intertwined with vines and branches, then plastered with mud.

WASG 550 AM & WYDH 105.9 FM

These Alabama Native American Broadcasting Company stations originate from Atmore. The stations air programs of interest to local Indians. Tune in!

Women

Indian women worked very hard and enjoyed many rights. In some tribes, women elected the chief. In other tribes, men hunted, and women did the rest of the work. Creek society was divided into at least 46 maternal clans. After birth, children were automatically part of the mother's clan. Thus clan membership was passed on through women.

War Club

A weapon made of stone, bone, or wood in the shape of a club.

War Bonnet

Special headdress worn into battle, often adorned with feathers.

Wampum

Algonquian word used to describe strings or belts of beads made of clam or whelk shells. Originally used as tribal records and message communicators to other tribes, they later became a form of money used between the Indians and settlers. In 1640, counterfeit wampum was made!

XYZ are for . . .

Y-tav-a

Indian town that existed during Hernando de Soto's exploration, which is present-day Duck Springs in Etowah County, near Gasden, Alabama.

Young Scarecrows

Choctaw children camped in small shelters near fields to chase crows away from the growing crops!

Yuchi

Southeast Indian tribe. The Yuchis were part of the Creek confederacy, but they spoke their own language and observed their own rituals. The Yuchis mostly worshipped the sun. Their light-skinned, blue-eyed, tall women looked very different from the other Creek Indians and were traditionally very desirable.

Yaupon

This holly tree's leaves were part of what went into the "black drink." Southern Indian tribesmen drank it for ceremonial cleansing and purification.

ZZZZZZ...

Shamans and medicine men were not the only people who had access to the spirit world. Indians believed that people could make contact with spirits every night in their dreams! Dreamers could travel back to the time of man's creation or far ahead into their own futures. They also believed that dreams contained warnings or commands from the spirits. Many tribes felt that they had to act out their dreams as soon as they awoke. If an Indian dreamed about bathing, for example, he would run to his neighbors' houses first thing in the morning, and his neighbors would throw kettles full of cold water over him.

Y... Or, "Why?"

1. Why do you think Indian warriors carried charms with them? Some Indian medicines have been scientifically proven to have true healing power and are still used today. Do you think their charms had any real power to help them win battles?
2. Why do you think the American government kept relocating Indians onto reservations and then making the reservations smaller and smaller?
3. Why did Indians use items such as a pipe in ceremonies? What kinds of symbolic objects do we use in ceremonies today?
4. Why and how did Indians use natural materials in creative ways?
5. Many Indian tribes are running successful businesses on their reservations today. There is one industry that many tribes are making a lot of money at. Do you know what this is? Hint: "I'll bet you do!"

Which Famous Native American Am I?

Solve the puzzle!

Down

1. This Shoshone woman joined Lewis and Clark as their guide and translator and helped make the expedition a success! Hint: She has 4 "a"s in her name!

4. This man gave the Cherokee their first alphabet so that they could write. Until then, they communicated only by speaking and drawing pictures. Hint: A famous ancient tree also has the same name!

5. He was one of the fiercest of Indian warriors! He fought against white settlers in Arizona and New Mexico to keep his people from being pushed off their lands. Hint: Jump!

Word Bank

Black Elk   Crazy Horse   Sitting Bull   Sequoia
Sacajawea   Chief Joseph   Geronimo   Pocahontas

Across

2. A legend says that this brave Algonquian woman saved the life of Englishman John Smith. Hint: Disney produced a movie about her.

3. He fought at Little Bighorn when he was only 13! He was also a wise "shaman" who saw visions and could advise people. Hint: Part of his name is an animal with antlers!

6. He was a great Sioux warrior who won the battle against General Custer at Little Bighorn in 1876. Hint: His horse was not crazy!

7. A leader of the Lakota (Sioux) tribe who lived on the Standing Rock Reservation in North Dakota after the battle of Little Bighorn. He tried to make conditions better for his people there, so the U.S. government called him a "troublemaker." Hint: He did not sit all the time!

8. A wise and brave chief of the Nez Percé who tried to bring his people to Canada to escape war. He said, "From where the sun now stands, I will fight no more forever." Hint: His father's name was "Old Joseph."

Different Ways for Different Indians!

North American Indian tribes are divided into different areas. In each of these areas, tribes shared common ways of living with each other. They might make similar arts or crafts, they might eat the same foods, or they might have had the same beliefs. These activities are all part of their "culture." Each area had its own culture, which was different from the tribes in all the other areas.

Below is a map of all the different groups of Indian tribes in North America. Color each area with a different color. You will see a colorful picture of how Native Americans can all be called "Indians" but still have very different cultures!

Celebration!

Powwows are big festivals where Native Americans gather to sing, dance, and eat together. It is a time to celebrate and show pride in their culture. Powwows can last from one afternoon to several days. The Indians dress in native costumes and dance ancient dances to the beating of drums.

Artists sell their arts and crafts. You might be able to buy some real Native American food cooked on an open fire. Native Americans go to powwows to be with each other, share ideas, and just have fun! Most powwows are also open to people who are not Indian. It's a great place to learn about Native American culture!

If you went to a powwow this weekend, what do you think you would see? What do you think might NOT be there? Circle the objects you think you would see at a powwow. Put an X through those you probably won't see.

Make an Indian Weaving!

Many Native Americans used weaving to create useful things like sashes (belts), bags, mats, and blankets. They used animal hair to make yarn, and dyed the yarn with natural dyes from fruits and other plants. They also used some plant fibers, like cotton, to make weaving thread.

Weave a small Native American mat of your own. Use different colors of yarn to create a beautiful pattern in your weaving. Place a favorite object on the mat or hang it on your wall!

Prepare the "loom"

Cut a piece of cardboard 5 inches wide and 6 inches long. Along the two 5-inch sides (the "short" sides), have an adult cut slits 1/4 inch deep. These slits should be 1/2 inch apart from each other. So, on each short side you will have 9 slits.

Directions:

1. Take a long piece of yarn and bring it from the back through the first slit (the one next to the edge of the cardboard.) The end of the yarn will hang down behind the cardboard.

2. Bring the yarn right across the front of the cardboard to the slit opposite the one your yarn came through.

3. Now bring the yarn under the back of the cardboard and then up again through the second slit.

4. Repeat #2 and #3, until you have 9 strands of yarn across the front of your cardboard!

5. Then cut the yarn and tie the two loose ends in the back of the cardboard.

6. Take another piece of yarn and start feeding it through the 9 strands, going over one, under the next over the next, etc. When you get to the end, pull the yarn behind the cardboard and around to the front, and begin again. This time, whatever strand you went over, go under. And whatever strand you went under, go over.

7. Repeat this pattern until the front of your cardboard in covered. Then cut the yarn in the back of the cardboard, and trim it to create a fringe for your mat!

Tips!
- For a wild look, use variegated or different colored yarn!
- For a tighter mat, push the under/over strands up against the previous strands during weaving.
- To keep your mat from unravelling, tie neighboring fringe together up close to the mat.

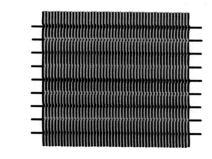

Finders Keepers?

Native Americans have many buried treasures. For hundreds of years, special objects would sometimes be buried with Native Americans, or maybe they would just be lost. Archeologists used to dig for interesting artifacts in old Native American gravesites. They would keep the Native American bones or the arrowheads, rattles, masks and other objects that they found. But this made the Native Americans feel like they were being robbed.

In 1990, the U.S. government passed a law that said that no one could look for or take these Native American objects anymore. And whoever had any already had to give them back to the people they belonged to. This is called repatriation

Help the archeologist return the artifact to a Native American.

FINISH

START

Fast Fact

An artifact is an object that was made by people a long time ago for some useful purpose.

Busy Hands!

Before modern times, Native Americans didn't have stores where they went to buy things. They made everything they needed.

What did Indians make with their own hands? Use the Word Bank and pictures to find out!

Word Bank

blanket	moccasins	arrows	pottery	canoe
mat	food	jewelry	pouch	box

_ _ _ _ _ _   _ _ _ _ _ _ _

_ _ _ _ _ _   _ _ _ _ _ _ _

_ _ _ _ _ _ _ _

_ _ _ _ _ _ _ _

_ _ _ _ _ _ _ _ _

_ _ _ _ _ _ _ _

_ _ _ _ _ _ _

_ _ _ _ _ _ _

34

American Indians Today

Beginning with the first letter of each group of letters, cross out every other letter to discover some new words. You may not have heard of these before, but you can read all about them!

1. Many Indians live on these, but many more do not!

TRYELSDEBRNVJAOTPIPOWNASX

_____

2. Many Indians have been poor for a long time because for many years the government took away their lands and their ability to make a living.

TPKOOVWEBRNTXYA

_____

3. Many Indians have been studying hard at school and going to college in order to earn more money. Education helps the Indians make their lives better. These Native Americans are working to become:

TSJUMCBCFEYSMSOFPUVL

_____

4. This is a big term that means Native Americans have worked hard to get the U.S. government to let them rule themselves. This means that they have their own laws and make their own decisions. They are like a separate country inside the U.S.! Now, try and see if you can get your parents to give you the same thing!

TSGENLBF   **JDGEETSEWRAMCIHNUAKTYIKOTNU**

_____   _____

Fast Fact

What do Indians work as today?

- doctors
- nurses
- factory workers
- artists
- lawyers
- actors

The same kinds of jobs any American might work at!

35

Native Americans Move to the City!

Solve the code to discover the mystery words!

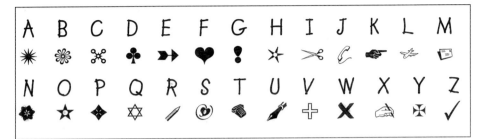

1. During the 1950s and 1960s, the American government paid Indians to leave their homes on reservations and move to cities to get jobs. If cities are sometimes called urban areas, then these brave Indians were called:

2. Many Indians chose to stay on their reservations and not move to the city. They thought that if they moved to the city, they would lose the way of life that their parents and ancestors had taught. These Indians called themselves:

3. Native Americans who moved to cities lived close to each other. They tried to keep their way of life as much as possible. They did not want to forget their religion, native art, or music. They did not want to lose their:

4. Are you afraid of heights? Many people are. The Mohawk Indians are not! Many of them work hundreds of feet above the city to build steel frames for skyscrapers. People who do this work above the city are:

5. Today urban Indians and reservation Indians come together to celebrate their culture. They share ideas and stories. They dance and beat drums. They make and sell Indian jewelry. During these celebrations, Indians remember how much they have to be proud of! These big parties are called

36